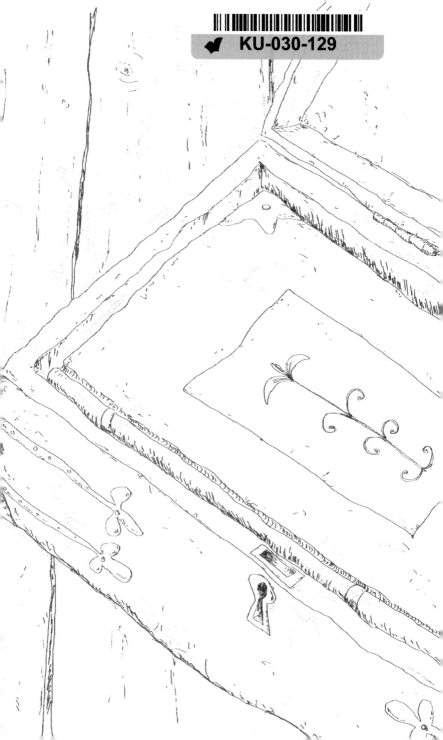

JOE O'BRIEN is an award-winning gardener who lives in Ballyfermot in Dublin. This is his fifth book about the wonderful world of Alfie Green. He has also written two books for older readers: *Little Croker* and *Féile Fever*.

DEDICATION

The *Alfie Green* series is dedicated to my son, Ethan, who in his short time in this world taught me to be strong, happy and thankful for the gift of life. Thank you, Ethan, for the inspiration to write.

Alfie Green and the Monkey Puzzler is dedicated to Jessica, Nicole, Lauren and Rebecca of St Catherine's Primary School, Cabra.

ACKNOWLEDGEMENTS:

A big thank you to all at The O'Brien Press, to Jean Texier, and, of course, to my readers.

*   *   *

JEAN TEXIER is a storyboard artist and illustrator. Initially trained in animation, he has worked in the film industry for many years.

Alfie
and the MONKEY PUZZLER
Green

Joe O'Brien

Illustrated by Jean Texier

THE O'BRIEN PRESS
DUBLIN

First published in hardback 2007 by The O'Brien Press Ltd.,
12 Terenure Road East, Rathgar, Dublin 6, Ireland.
Tel: +353 1 4923333; Fax: +353 1 4922777
E-mail: books@obrien.ie
Website: www.obrien.ie
This paperback edition first published 2009.

ISBN: 978-1-84717-174-0

British Library Cataloguing-in-Publication Data
A catalogue record for this title is available from The British Library

2 3 4 5 6 7 8 9 10
09 10 11 12

The O'Brien Press receives
assistance from

Editing, typesetting, layout, design: The O'Brien Press Ltd.
Illustrations: Jean Texier

CONTENTS

CHAPTER 1 WHAT'S THAT NOISE? PAGE 8

CHAPTER 2 A FREE CIRCUS! 15

CHAPTER 3 THE SHOW BEGINS 22

CHAPTER 4 POOR MR BOGGINS! 27

CHAPTER 5 OOPS! 36

CHAPTER 6 ROBBERS IN THE HOUSE 46

CHAPTER 7 THE MONKEY PUZZLER 54

CHAPTER 8 ALFIE'S CHALLENGE 60

CHAPTER 9 THE BIG PRIZE 68

CHAPTER 1

WHAT'S THAT NOISE?

Alfie Green was in his back garden, mowing the lawn. His grandad's old mower was so loud that he had to use earmuffs to keep out the noise.

Suddenly Alfie noticed all the plants swaying from side to side, as if they were dancing.

He turned off the machine and took off the earmuffs. He heard music. There were trumpets and drums and whistles …

Alfie raced around to the front of the house.

His mother and his granny were at the gate, clapping and cheering. All the neighbours were there too, including Mrs Butler and Old Podge Kelly.

It was a circus parade, but not like any circus Alfie had seen before.

The floats were driven by circus people but all the performers were **MONKEYS**.

There were monkey acrobats and monkey clowns. And the music was being played by a monkey band.

Fitzer spotted Alfie and ran over to him.

'This is **nuts**, isn't it, Alfie?'

'Yes,' Alfie agreed. 'Monkey nuts!' The two pals burst out laughing.

As the last float passed by, the music stopped and a man with a tall hat and a loudspeaker rode up on a unicycle.

'Ladies and gentlemen, boys and girls,' he called, 'For one night only, come and see Monty's Marvellous Monkey Circus. Seven o'clock, at Budsville Primary School playing field. Free admission. Yes! That's right, **FREE!** Just bring along your leaflets.'

A gang of really small monkeys jumped off the back of a float. They ran over to the crowd and handed out leaflets to everyone.

'Ah, isn't that cute,' Mrs Butler said, and a little monkey in a clown suit jumped up on her shoulder and gave her a big kiss.

'**Aaaaaagh**,' she screamed. 'You cheeky monkey!'

CHAPTER 2

A FREE CIRCUS!

Alfie and Fitzer sat on the footpath long after the circus parade had disappeared up the road.

'I wonder why it's free?' Alfie asked.

'Who cares?' Fitzer said. 'Did you see the prices for Dumbkins' Circus on the other side of town? Hey! Look at this! It says on the leaflet that if we fill in our names and addresses we could win a BIG PRIZE.'

'Nice one,' Alfie said. They ran over to Fitzer's house to get a pen.

That night, Alfie and Fitzer headed off to the circus really early to be sure of getting a ringside seat. But when they reached the school there was a long line of people ahead of them.

'It looks like the whole of Budsville is going to the circus,' Fitzer said.

It took Alfie and Fitzer twenty minutes to get to the top of the queue. A tall, skinny, scruffy-looking man in a dusty black suit took their leaflets. He put them into a bag being held by a small monkey who sat on his shoulder.

Suddenly Whacker Walsh appeared at their side.

'Sorry I'm late, lads,' Whacker shouted, pretending that Alfie and Fitzer were waiting for him.

Alfie wanted to tell the circus man that Whacker had skipped the queue, but the man didn't look too friendly, so Alfie said nothing.

As soon as they got inside the tent, Alfie and Fitzer found two really good seats.

Whacker spotted Mercedes Devine, a girl from Alfie's class, and sat next to her, in the seat in front of Fitzer.

Mercedes didn't look too pleased, but Alfie and Fitzer were delighted that he wasn't sitting with them.

'Wow!' Alfie gasped as he looked around.

Sparkling lights in all the colours of the rainbow hung down from the high roof of the striped tent. There were flags and balloons and paper lanterns. The circus ring was covered in sand and there were hoops and barrels and seesaws for the monkeys to do tricks on.

It was magic!

CHAPTER 3

THE SHOW BEGINS

Because the circus was free, Alfie and Fitzer could spend their pocket money on goodies. They bought huge tubs of popcorn, big sticks of candyfloss and giant fizzy orange drinks.

Tar-An-Tar-Aaaa

At seven o'clock exactly the monkey band blew their trumpets and banged their drums.

Monty, the circus owner, cycled into the ring.

'Welcome to Monty's Marvellous Monkey Circus. Let the show begin!'

There were monkeys juggling balls and plastic bananas. Monkeys driving toy cars. There were flying trapeze monkeys and even a monkey in a pink dress dancing across a tightrope high up near the roof of the tent.

It was the best circus ever.

After the monkey acrobats had finished their act, Monty came back into the ring.

'Now, ladies and gentlemen, boys and girls, it's time for some lucky person to win the Big Prize.'

He clapped his hands twice, and two monkeys pushed a drum out into the centre of the ring. Monty put his hand into the drum and pulled out a leaflet.

CHAPTER 4

POOR MR BOGGINS!

'Do we have a Barnaby Boggins in the audience?' Monty asked.

Principal Boggins tried to hide, but Whacker Walsh stood up and pointed, 'There he is!,' he shouted.

Principal Boggins was led down to the centre of the ring by one of the juggling monkeys.

'Welcome, Mr Boggins,' Monty said with a big smile. 'Now, all you have to do to collect your Big Prize is to give Edison here a challenge that he can't solve.'

The spotlight shone on a very large monkey in a navy pinstriped suit.

'Ladies and gentlemen, boys and girls, meet the most intelligent ape in the world. The one, the only, Edison, the genius.'

Edison bowed gracefully and the whole crowd cheered.

Alfie was disappointed. Principal Boggins was probably the smartest person in Budsville.

'It's no contest,' he said. 'Boggins will win. I wonder what his Big Prize will be?'

Monty explained to the crowd that Mr Boggins had only one chance to outsmart Edison. If he succeeded he would win the Big Prize, but if he failed he would have to do a forfeit.

Principal Boggins looked a bit worried, and then he thought, well, how intelligent can a monkey be?

He knelt down on the sand in the ring and began to write lots of figures. It was a very hard sum indeed.

'I challenge Edison to solve this equation,' said Mr Boggins.

Edison shuffled over to the spot and looked down. Then he bent over and drew a long line of squiggles in the sand.

Principal Boggins' face turned pink, then bright red.

'I'm afraid he's right,' he admitted.

'Ladies and gentlemen, Edison WINS!'

Monty lifted Edison's arm over his head. Then he gave him a huge bunch of bananas as a reward.

'Hurray! Hurray!' The crowd clapped and cheered.

'Poor Boggins,' laughed Fitzer, 'I can't believe he was outsmarted by a monkey!'

'Hard luck, Mr Boggins,' Monty said. 'You lose, so you must pay a forfeit.'

Three monkeys came out into the centre of the ring. Two of them were riding small tricycles and the third carried a skirt and a big pair of frilly knickers.

'Now, Mr Boggins,' Monty said, laughing, 'You must put on the skirt and knickers and race Samson around the ring.'

CHAPTER 5

OOPS!

At first Principal Boggins refused, but one look at Samson's frown and he quickly put on the frilly knickers and the skirt and hopped onto the tricycle.

He started to pedal. But his legs were too long and his lumpy knees bumped off the handlebars

It was **HILARIOUS**.

Then Whacker Walsh began to shout, 'SAM - SON! SAM - SON!', and the crowd joined in.

Soon Alfie was feeling sorry for Principal Boggins. And he *really* didn't like Whacker Walsh.

Alfie jumped up to cheer for Mr Boggins.

OOPS! He knocked against Fitzer's elbow and sent the giant paper cup of fizzy orange fly**ing** out of his hand.

It landed straight on Whacker Walsh's head.

Whacker was totally drenched. Rivers of orange ran off his hair and into his eyes. He jumped up, shaking his head like a shaggy dog coming out of the water.

Big orange drops splashed all over Mercedes' new dress.

Mercedes began to cry.

Whacker turned around slowly and gave Fitzer a look that you only see in horror movies.

'You're **dead meat**, Fitzpatrick!'

'Time to go, Fitzer,' Alfie yelled. The two pals dodged through the rows of seating and raced out of the tent, followed by Whacker.

'Quick, Fitzer,' Alfie gasped. 'Behind the wagon.'

They hid behind a circus wagon that was parked near the school gate.

'We're safe here,' Alfie whispered, as he watched Whacker peering through the darkness in search of them.

Then a huge shadow fell over the wagon.

'**WHAT** are you two up to?'

Alfie and Fitzer nearly jumped out of their skins.

It was the scruffy circus man who had collected the leaflets. He was holding a small monkey by the hand. In his other hand was a large brown bag.

Tick-TOCK ... Tick-TOCK ... Alfie could hear a loud ticking coming from the bag.

That's strange, he thought.

'You brats are not allowed near the wagon,' the man yelled angrily. 'Now clear off!'

Alfie and Fitzer burst from their hiding place.

'There you are,' shouted Whacker.

CHAPTER 6

ROBBERS IN THE HOUSE

When they reached the Greens' house, Fitzer and Alfie were gasping for breath.

Alfie's hand shook as he tried to turn the key in the lock.

Fitzer could hear Whacker pounding up the street. 'Hurry, Alfie. Hurry!'

They had just banged the door shut when Whacker arrived at the gate.

'I'll get you, Fitzpatrick, if I have to wait here all night,' shouted Whacker.

After a few minutes, Alfie peeped out through the curtains. Whacker was still there, but the fizzy orange had become sticky and his hair was itchy. He turned around and made a horrible face at Alfie. Then he jumped off the wall and headed home to wash his hair.

'Good news, Fitzer, Whacker's gone,' said Alfie.

He was about to close the curtains when he noticed something strange.

A little monkey was climbing down the drainpipe of Fitzer's house. When he got to the ground he ran off, a full-looking bag hanging from his neck.

As Alfie looked down the street, he saw another monkey jumping over Mr Skully's wall. At the bottom of the road a man was collecting bags from other monkeys.

'Of course,' Alfie said, 'That's why the circus was free!'

'What are you on about, Alfie?' Fitzer was puzzled.

'The monkeys from the circus are robbing the houses.'

'The monkeys are **WHAT**?'

'It was all a trick, Fitzer,' Alfie explained. 'Monty wanted to get everyone to come to the circus so he could rob their houses while they were out. That's why it was free. And he knew which houses were empty because the names and addresses were on the back of the leaflets!'

'Shhh!' Fitzer said suddenly. 'Listen. Did you hear that?'

There was a patter of feet on the stairs – small feet.

'There's a monkey robber in the house!' Alfie whispered.

In a split second Fitzer set the world record for disappearing into the small cupboard under the stairs.

There was no room for Alfie.

CHAPTER 7

THE MONKEY PUZZLER

Time for a bit of special help, Alfie thought. He ran out to the shed, lifted the loose floorboard and took out the magical book that his grandad had left him.

Alfie placed his hand on the seed on the first page and the wise old plant rose up from the book.

'It's a bit late, isn't it, Alfie?' said the wise old plant, yawning.

Alfie told him about the circus, and the robber monkeys, and Edison.

'Hmmm,' said the wise old plant. 'Is the circus over?'

'No,' Alfie said, 'We had to leave before the end.'

The wise old plant began to flick through the pages of the magical book until he came to the place that said 'The Monkey Puzzler'.

Alfie saw monkeys standing around the bottom of a tall tree, scratching their heads.

'I know that tree!' Alfie said. 'There's one in the school grounds, right beside the circus tent.'

The wise old plant told Alfie to go back to the circus and challenge Edison.

'Me! Challenge Edison? Why? How?'

'The minute the circus is over, Monty and his helpers will pack up and leave,' the wise old plant explained.

'You will have to keep them busy until the police arrive, Alfie. Tell Monty you want to challenge Edison, and then bring Edison out to that tree.'

'Then what?'

'Just ask the tree why it's called a "monkey puzzler",' the wise old plant smiled.

He plucked a blue hair from a leaf and handed it to Alfie.

'Here's a little bit of magic to help you with the other monkeys, just in case things get out of hand.'

Then he folded himself back into
the book, which closed with a

CHAPTER 8

ALFIE'S CHALLENGE

Alfie crept back into his house and found Fitzer in the hall.

'They're gone, Alfie,' Fitzer said.

'Right,' Alfie told him, 'Here's the plan. You go and get the police. I'll meet you all back at the circus. Hurry!'

When Alfie got back to the tent, Monty was thanking everyone for coming to the show.

'Wait!' Alfie shouted, and he rushed into the centre of the ring. 'I want to challenge Edison.'

Everyone laughed.

'I'm afraid the circus is over, little boy,' said Monty.

'I'm not a little boy,' Alfie said crossly.

He turned to the crowd. 'He's *afraid* to let me challenge Edison.'

A voice from the crowd shouted, 'Let him challenge the monkey!'

It was old Podge Kelly.

Way to go, Mr Kelly! Alfie thought.

Monty was furious, but he pretended to smile.

'Of course he can challenge Edison! Now, what's your challenge, young man?'

Alfie led the way outside, followed by Monty and Edison and the whole crowd. When he got to the tree he leaned over and whispered, 'Why are you called a monkey puzzler?'

The Monkey Puzzler laughed. 'Just ask a monkey to climb to my top branch,' it said.

Alfie didn't like the sound of this. After all, climbing trees was what monkeys did best.

64

Alfie announced his challenge.

'I challenge Edison to climb to the top of this tree,' he shouted.

The crowd started laughing.

Uh-oh, thought Old Podge.

'Go on, Edison,' said Monty.

Edison shuffled his way over to the Monkey Puzzler and wrapped his arms and legs around the trunk. He reached for a branch. Then he dropped to the ground, holding his hand and screeching in pain. He sat looking up at the tree and scratching his head.

'You see, Alfie,' said the Monkey Puzzler. 'He'll never figure out how to climb up through my sharp, pointy leaves. Now you know why I'm called a monkey puzzler.'

Alfie had outsmarted Edison with the simplest task that a monkey could be asked to do.

CHAPTER 9

THE BIG PRIZE

Just then Fitzer arrived with the police.

'Now then,' said the police chief to Monty. 'What have you been up to? And where are these robber monkeys we've been told about?'

'They must be hiding in the circus wagons,' Alfie said. 'You should search there.'

'Psst! Psst!' The Monkey Puzzler was trying to get Alfie's attention. 'They're in the tree beside me,' he called out to Alfie.

Alfie blew softly on the blue hair that the wise old plant had given him. It rose up, spun around a few times, and then turned into a sparkling blue banana.

The banana whirled through the branches of the tree.

Out fell ...

ONE,

  TWO,

    THREE ...

... a whole **GANG** of small monkeys, clutching big brown bags.

As they landed on the ground, the bags burst open, and rings, watches, necklaces, clocks and money tumbled onto the grass.

The police arrested Monty and his helpers, and congratulated Alfie and Fitzer for exposing Monty's

Marvellous Monkey Circus for what it really was: a circus of **thieves**.

'What's going to happen to the monkeys?' Alfie asked. 'They were only doing what they were trained to do.'

'I'll take them,' said a voice.

A small round man dressed in a bright red coat stepped out from the crowd.

'Who are you?' Alfie asked.

'Jack Dumbkins, of Dumbkins' Dazzling Circus.'

Fitzer nudged Alfie. 'That's the really expensive circus across town.'

'I heard about this free circus,' Mr Dumbkins continued, 'And I thought I'd come along to see it for myself. I'd be happy to take the monkeys and retrain them.'

Fitzer remembered something.

'Hey, Alfie! You never got your Big Prize for outsmarting Edison!'

'Aha!' said Mr Dumbkins. He reached into his pocket and handed Alfie two tickets to Dumbkins' Dazzling Circus.

Dumbkins'
Dazzling Circus
FRONT ROW TICKETS

Looks like Alfie Green got his BIG
PRIZE after all!

READ ALFIE'S OTHER GREAT ADVENTURES IN:

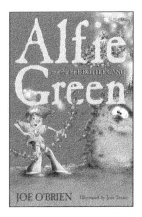

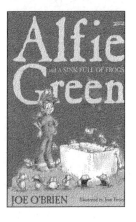

ALFIE GREEN AND THE MAGICAL GIFT
ALFIE GREEN AND A SINK FULL OF FROGS
ALFIE GREEN AND THE BEE-BOTTLE GANG
ALFIE GREEN AND THE FLY-TRAPPER

ALFIE GREEN AND THE CONKER KING
ALFIE GREEN AND THE SUPERSONIC SUBWAY
ALFIE GREEN AND THE SNOWDROP QUEEN

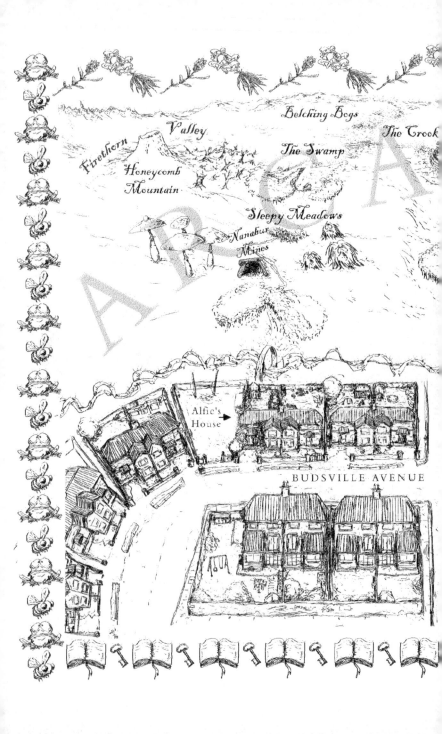

The
Wonderful World of
Alfie Green

SYCAMORE ROAD

LAUREL PARK

BUDSVILLE
PRIMARY
SCHOOL

PRAISE FOR THE
ALFIE GREEN SERIES

'Gorgeous books, beautifully illustrated.'

Sunday Independent

'Readers will hang on every word.'

BookFest 2008

'A great choice for boys and girls.'

Irish Independent

'Bright, breezy and full of flesh crawling incidents. Young readers will love this.'

Village

'Best writer ever.' Siobhan Quigley (age 8)

Laois Voice